Patrick Duck

Books by L. Sydney Abel

Gruvel the Great
Ish-ish Ishbochernay
Keypya and the Pirates
Kingsley Trunk
Marge and the Wobbly Onkey
Mr. Runkin's Secret
Patrick Duck
Smelly Nelly Welly
The Evergreen Wolf

Patrick Duck

L. Sydney Abel

SPEAKING VOLUMES, LLC
NAPLES, FLORIDA
2018

Patrick Duck

ISBN 978-1-62815-502-0

This book is for

The little girl who heard it first

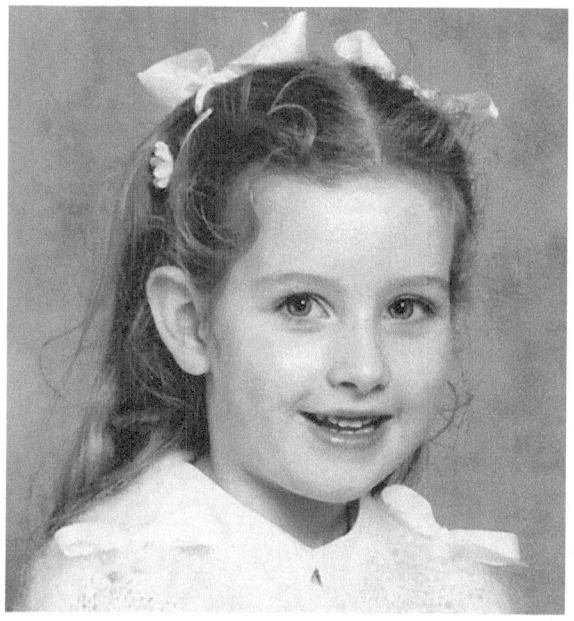

Thank you Karen for your patience and understanding

Table of Contents

Our Story Begins

Where pigs roll in the mud and cows eat grass all day, a holly tree grows in the garden of a cottage. The cottage is called Holly Cottage and it is the home of Mr. and Mrs. Butterworth.

Next to Holly Cottage is Butterworth Farm, where lots of animals live. There are horses, pigs, goats and ducks, and also lots of noisy chickens.

The chickens like to sit on the henhouse roof and watch everything that happens.

Quack 1 the new arrivals

This is the story of Patrick Duck

Butterworth Farm was very quiet as everyone waited for a new arrival.

Cries of joy came from Holly Cottage as Mrs. Butterworth cradled a baby girl. Mr. Butterworth smiled seeing Mrs. Butterworth give her daughter her first kiss and cuddle.

Mrs. Butterworth named their daughter 'Leanne'. There was no reason other than she liked the name. Mr. Butterworth agreed.

At the same time, on the farm, a new duckling hatched from his egg.

When Mrs. Butterworth saw the duckling she named him after her grandfather for good luck.

Every morning she would hold the little duckling and feed him and say, "How's Patrick this morning?" Then she would feed all the other ducks.

All the other ducks became jealous of Patrick and stopped talking to him.

Every morning, at breakfast, Mr. Butterworth would look at Leanne and say, "Hello, little buttercup. How much is my butter worth?"

Mrs. Butterworth would smile and coo at Leanne.

The little buttercup would giggle.

Quack 2 a year later

This is the story of Patrick Duck
Who was given his name for good luck

Patrick quickly grew. It wasn't long before he was playing with the other animals.

It had rained heavily, making the farmyard very wet. Patrick liked to paddle in the puddles. He chased the chickens to make them run and cluck.

The chickens didn't mind being in Patrick's game; they liked running and clucking.

In the late afternoon, Patrick watched Farmer Butterworth bring home the cows from the fields and lead them into the milking sheds.

Each cow said, "Hello," to Patrick, as they passed him standing by the gate.

"What's beyond the fields–Quack, quack?" asked Patrick.

"More fields–Moo, moo," answered the cows.

"And what's beyond more fields–Quack, quack?" asked Patrick.

"Maybe more fields–Moo, moo," answered the cows. "Why-Moo?"

"I just wondered–Quack, quack," said Patrick.

Patrick had seen other ducks leave the farm in a truck. They never returned. He wanted to know where they went.

When Mr. Butterworth came in for his tea, he picked Leanne up and said, "How big are we today?"

Leanne stretched out her arms and wiggled them like flippers.

Mrs. Butterworth smiled and said, "So big!"

The little flipper wiggled and giggled.

Quack 3 leaving the farm

This is the story of Patrick Duck
Who was given his name for good luck
He chased the chickens and made them cluck

Patrick waddled around a wet and muddy farmyard. He went to see the pigs, the horses, and the goats.

"What's beyond the fields–Quack, quack?" he asked them all.

"Why–Oink?–Neigh?–Meh?" they asked.

"I just wondered," answered Patrick.

"We're happy here–Oink, oink," said the pigs, as they rolled around in the mud.

"We like it here–Neigh, neigh," said the horses, as they ran and jumped around their paddock.

"We can eat what we want–Meh, meh," said the goats, as they chewed on Farmer Butterworth's hat.

Patrick had an idea. He decided to go and see for himself what was beyond the fields. He went out of the gate and waddled down the lane. He waddled past Holly Cottage. The sun came out from behind the clouds; it was softly warming the animals and trying hard to dry the ground.

Mrs. Butterworth was in the garden, hanging out the washing.

Mr. Butterworth was holding Leanne by the hands as she tottered along learning to walk.

Mr. Butterworth looked at Leanne and said, "To walk you have to try. If you fall down try not to cry."

Mrs. Butterworth smiled and nodded in agreement.

The little totterer chuckled.

Quack 4 chicken warning

This is the story of Patrick Duck
Who was given his name for good luck
He chased the chickens and made them cluck
Beyond the fields he would go and look

Patrick waddled further down the lane. He wondered where it led. How he hoped it would take him beyond the fields, so he could see what was there.

Along the lane came a very large truck. It was travelling towards Butterworth Farm. The lane was full of puddles.

Onto the henhouse flapped all the chickens-they had seen the silly duck leave the farmyard and go down the lane. They saw the truck.

"Patrick, get out of the way-Cluck, cluck, cluck," cried the chickens.

Patrick didn't hear the chickens and he didn't see the truck.

Mrs. Butterworth sat on a garden chair, enjoying a nice cup of tea.

Mr. Butterworth fed Leanne her dinner. He looked at Leanne and said, "Here comes the aeroplane. Open the doors and let it in." He flew the spoon in the air, up and down and round and round.

Leanne shuffled and shook her head. Then she opened her mouth to let the plane in.

Mrs. Butterworth said, "Good girl."

The little shuffler said, "All gone!"

Quack 5 a duck in danger

This is the story of Patrick Duck
Who was given his name for good luck
He chased the chickens and made them cluck
Beyond the fields he would go and look
To Butterworth Farm travelled a very large truck

Patrick stopped in the lane and looked back at Butterworth Farm.

From where he stood he could see Leanne waving her arms. He realised he had never been this far away from home before.

All the clucking made the pigs stop rolling in the mud.

All the clucking made the horses stop running and jumping around their paddock.

All the clucking even made the goats stop chewing another of Mr. Butterworth's hats.

The pigs, the horses, and the goats looked at the chickens. They wondered what all the clucking was for.

The driver of the truck whistled along to a song on the radio. He didn't see Patrick standing in the lane. The wheels of his truck splashed through puddles of muck.

Mr. Butterworth picked Leanne up and popped her on his shoulders. He ran around the garden pretending that she had disappeared and he couldn't find her.

Mrs. Butterworth heard the chickens clucking and wondered what was wrong.

Mr. Butterworth said to Leanne, "It's what chickens do when they're not in their coop. Chicken is best when it's made into soup."

Leanne didn't giggle, wiggle or chuckle.

Mrs. Butterworth didn't say anything. Instead, she gave Mr. Butterworth a very stern look.

The little vanisher pointed to Patrick and said, "Quack! Quack!"

Quack 6 — crash!

This is the story of Patrick Duck
Who was given his name for good luck
He chased the chickens and made them cluck
Beyond the fields he would go and look
To Butterworth Farm travelled a very large truck
Its wheels splashed through puddles of muck

Patrick heard splashing and rumbling. He turned and suddenly saw the very large truck. He flapped his wings in fright.

There was a squeal of brakes.

There was an almighty bump.

There was a very loud CRACK.

Mud went everywhere.

The chickens stopped clucking with shock. The pigs, the horses, and the goats were shocked. Mr. and Mrs. Butterworth, and Leanne were shocked.

The truck had swerved and was stuck in a hole full of water. The engine's radiator had cracked and sent steam hissing into the air.

Patrick stood just inches away. He was covered from head to tail-feather in yuck.

Mr. and Mrs. Butterworth, and Leanne rushed to see what had happened. They saw a broken-down truck stuck in a very deep puddle. They also saw a dripping wet duck covered in muck.

The driver was standing by his truck, shaking his head.

Leanne cried.

Mr. Butterworth looked at Leanne and said, "No harm done. Patrick's alright. He's just wet and dirty."

Leanne stopped crying and waved at Patrick.

Mrs. Butterworth looked at Patrick and said, "You're a very lucky duck."

The little tear-shedder said, "Mucky duck."

Quack 7 back to the farm

This is the story of Patrick Duck
Who was given his name for good luck
He chased the chickens and made them cluck
Beyond the fields he would go and look
To Butterworth Farm travelled a very large truck
Its wheels splashed through puddles of muck
Poor Patrick Duck got covered in yuck

Patrick was brought back to the farm. He felt very silly. If he had been any further down the lane he might not be here at all.

Mrs. Butterworth washed all the dirt from his feathers and said, "What a silly duck you are. You were meant to always stay at the farm and be safe from harm".

Patrick flapped his wings and quacked.

"So what's beyond the fields–Oink, oink?" asked the pigs from their sty, mud-rolling and nosey to know.

"I don't care. I'm happy here–Quack, quack," answered Patrick.

"So what's beyond the fields-Neigh, neigh?" asked the horses from their paddock, running and jumping and nosey to know.

"I don't care. I like it here-Quack, quack," answered Patrick.

"So what's beyond the fields-Meh, meh?" asked the goats, pushing their heads through the rails of the fence, all nosey to know.

"Just more fields-Quack, quack," answered Patrick.

Mr. Butterworth got his tractor and towed the truck to the garage for repair.

Mrs. Butterworth took Leanne to see Patrick.

Leanne and Patrick chased the chickens.

The chickens liked having Patrick back. They also liked Leanne making them run and cluck.

Mrs. Butterworth looked at Leanne and said, "Be careful-you don't want to get wet and dirty like a silly duck."

The cheeky chicken-chaser said, "Quack, quack, quack" and "Cluck, cluck, cluck."

"Silly duck-Cluck, cluck," said the chickens.

Patrick knew he was a very lucky duck!

L. Sydney Abel

This is the story of Patrick Duck
Who was given his name for good luck
He chased the chickens and made them cluck
Beyond the fields he would go and look
To Butterworth Farm travelled a very large truck
Its wheels splashed through puddles of muck
Poor Patrick Duck got covered in yuck
Patrick knew he was a very lucky duck!

How did Gruvel come to be on the Gregorys' doorstep?

Where has Gruvel come from?

And what on earth are they going to do with Gruvel?

As the family try to answer these questions,
Gruvel teaches them a wonderful lesson.

For more information
visit: www.speakingvolumes.us

One morning, whilst getting out of bed, a voice
whispered the name 'Kingsley Trunk' into my ear.
I always pay attention to my whisperer,
whoever that may be...

Kingsley
Trunk

Written and Illustrated by
L. Sydney Abel

For more information
visit: www.speakingvolumes.us

I'd like to go back in time, to put hurtful wrongs to right.
My advice: make time for the ones you love

A donkey, a letter, and a bottle of clear liquid
all combine to make 'The Secret'.

For more information
visit: www.speakingvolumes.us

One evening, my whisperer said the name 'Arthur Runkin'.
My imagination was alight!

Imagine knowing something about yourself.
And all because of a suitcase.

Mr. Runkin's
Secret

ARTHUR RUNKIN'S
AMAZING
FLEA CIRCUS

Written and Illustrated by
L. Sydney Abel

Published by SpeakingVolumes

For more information
visit: www.speakingvolumes.us

Can wolves change colour?

Do pixies exist?

According to Mr. Hedges they do.

Written and Illustrated by
L. Sydney Abel

For more information
visit: www.speakingvolumes.us

**Daydreaming about pirate adventures transports
'Then' to 'Now'**

**Sleepin' be one thing an' dreamin' be another.
But when dreamin' walks into yer wakin'
then that be something altogether diff'rent.**

For more information
visit: www.speakingvolumes.us

Under Nelida Wellington's stairs lives a Jinny-Yen.
Only children can see such creatures.
A Jinny-Yen is a Wish Granter.

And for most boys and girls, their thoughts turn to greed.
But not all children are devoured by greed…

Written and Illustrated by
L. Sydney Abel

For more information
visit: www.speakingvolumes.us